First Time

Meg Tilly

orca soundings

Orca Book Publishers

Library and Archives Canada Cataloguing in Publication

Tilly, Meg, 1960-

First Time / written by Meg Tilly.

(Orca soundings)
ISBN 978-1-55143-946-4 (bound) ISBN 978-1-55143-944-0 (pbk.)

I. Title. II. Series.
PS8589.I54F57 2008   jC813'.54   C2008-903025-7

Summary: Sixteen-year-old Haley must deal with unwanted
advances from her mother's new boyfriend.

First published in the United States, 2008
Library of Congress Control Number: 2008928551

Orca Book Publishers gratefully acknowledges the support for its publishing
programs provided by the following agencies: the Government of Canada
through the Book Publishing Industry Development Program and the Canada
Council for the Arts, and the Province of British Columbia through the BC
Arts Council and the Book Publishing Tax Credit.

Cover design by Teresa Bubela
Cover photography by Getty Images

ORCA BOOK PUBLISHERS
PO Box 5626, STN. B
VICTORIA, BC CANADA
V8R 6S4

ORCA BOOK PUBLISHERS
PO Box 468
CUSTER, WA USA
98240-0468

www.orcabook.com
Printed and bound in Canada.
Printed on 100% PCW recycled paper.

11 10 09 08 • 5 4 3 2 1

*To all of us whose first times
were less than perfect.*

Acknowledgments:

I'd like to thank my husband, Don, for his tireless
help and encouragement with all my writing. Bob
Tyrrell, the publisher of Orca Books, for asking me to
do one. I feel there is a real need for these types of
books and am proud to be part of the Soundings series.
Andrew Wooldridge, for his sensitive editing and brave
championing of interesting, relevant-to-teens material.
Teresa Bubela, for designing a thought-provoking
cover. And Dayle Sutherland, for all her tireless work,
getting the word out about Soundings books.

Meg Tilly is a former actress and a best-
selling novelist. *First Time* is her first
time being published by Orca. Meg lives
in Vancouver, British Columbia.

Chapter One

Standing at the end of our drive waiting for...get this...Lynn to pick me up in her *car*! *Her* car. She called me up on her cell phone twenty minutes ago. She was just pulling out of the Metro Toyota dealership in Victoria. And yes, I know, my driving instructor would say, "Talking on a cell phone while driving is unsafe behavior," but she just *bought* herself a car, for Christ's sake! She's gotta talk to somebody, and who better than me? Of course she had to call me.

So here I am, waiting for Lynn. Wondering if I have time to go back inside and get the lavender zip-up Juicy sweatshirt I scored at the after-Christmas sales. I doubt she'll be able to get back to Sooke so fast, even going the speed limit. Not only that, but this wind seems to be picking up a bit, and the sweatshirt seems like a two-girls-riding-around-town kind of ensemble. It's a casual, innocent, sexy look. There's something about the way it fits that makes me look more well-endowed than I am, and then it has that ribbing that makes my waist look really small.

That decides it. I sprint back up the drive, climb the porch steps, dart through the kitchen. I don't bother taking my runners off because I'm in a hurry. Besides, there's nobody at home to give me hell. At least that's what I think, until I pass by the den and see a movement inside. I get that tingly jolt of adrenaline for a second.

It's Larry, my mom's fancy new lawyer boyfriend, sitting behind mom's desk, a bunch of papers spread out before him. According to Sondra, Mom's best friend, "He's everything a woman could want in a man. He's smart, funny, rich and handsome. He's the whole package." And I suppose, if you're a middle-aged woman, perhaps he is all that. My mom's been really happy ever since they started dating, so I'm glad for her. It's just, I don't feel that comfortable around him. I want to like him, but I don't. I wish she hadn't given him the key.

"Hey, Haley," he says, standing up. He's got his tie loosened and his suit jacket hanging over the back of the chair. "Where are you off to in such a hurry?"

"Can't talk," I say, keeping my legs moving. "Lynn's waiting for me." I don't wait for his answer. I'm not trying to be rude, but I don't like hanging around him, especially when Mom's not home. There's something about him that gives me the creeps. Luckily he doesn't follow me.

Last week he did, right into my bedroom. Can you believe that? Hands casually slung in his slacks, dress shirt sleeves rolled up, leaning in my doorway, like he thinks he's some kind of male model in a Brooks Brothers ad. Had some sort of bogus excuse about wanting to see the painting I did in art class. Like I would show it to him.

I find my sweatshirt in the pile of clothes by my bed. That's where I keep my favorites. Easy access. Don't have to dig through all the mounds of stuff on my floor. Drives my mom nuts, how I have my room laid out. But really, she doesn't understand. It may look chaotic, but it's actually quite organized.

Back down the stairs, through the house, don't glance in Larry's direction, even though he's in the hallway now. I give him a wide berth, make a bit of a half circle. I don't know why. Maybe it's because I don't like him in my airspace. I fly out the kitchen door and am halfway down the porch steps when my cell phone rings. It's Lynn.

"I'm almost there," she says. "Just passing the gas station. Are you out front?" It's hard to hear her over the music she's got blasting.

"Almost." I'm running full tilt down the drive. "I'm almost there. Okay! I'm here. What should I look for? What color's your car?"

"White," she says. "It's a white 2002 Toyota Echo."

"Wow! That sounds great." Even though I have no idea what a Toyota Echo is. And I have to say, I'm kind of stunned that out of all the color choices there are in the world, she chose something as boring as white.

Just as I'm thinking that, I spot her car coming down the road. It's the pounding music that gives it away. I never noticed before, but there are a lot of white cars on the road.

"Whoohooo!" I yell, pumping both fists like she just made the winning score for the team. She leans on her horn. Her horn works well. It's good and loud. Heads turn, that's for sure. I'm waving, she's waving. She's got the windows of her car wide open, her auburn hair swirling around her, sunglasses on, a big smile on her face. She looks so grown up.

I get scared for a moment. It's weird. Doesn't make sense. I mean, she's my friend. She's bought a car. This is exciting. Something she's been saving for. So why do I feel like somebody punched me in the gut? Like it's the beginning of the end and she's outgrown me already, just doesn't know it yet. I should have brought my sunglasses too.

Chapter Two

"Hop in," she says, just like a character in a book or movie. I open the door and get in.

"This is totally awesome!" I say, and we smile at each other as she pulls out. I strap in, but I do it casually, like an afterthought, so it doesn't look like I don't trust her driving skills.

We are sailing down the road, free as birds, and now that I'm inside, the music is so loud it's vibrating the fillings in my teeth. I have to admit, I misjudged this car. It doesn't seem staid to me at all anymore. Not one bit. The air inside is electrified. We've just entered a whole new world. The world of people who ride in cars without parents, and I'm glad I've got my good-luck sweatshirt on.

"Where shall we go?" Lynn asks. She really does look like a movie star. It's like somebody sprinkled that extra something over her that she didn't have before. An extra something that I don't have. I feel awkward, sort of tongue-tied, which is ridiculous. This is Lynn. We've been best friends since eighth grade, for crying out loud.

"Um..." I say. I can't come up with a single stupid idea. "I don't know, what do you think?" How lame is that?

"Haley," Lynn says, giving me that look.

"Um..." I think fast, unglue my brain. "How about Dairy Queen?"

"Okay." Lynn shrugs. "Dairy Queen it is then." She jerks the steering wheel hard. Pulls a U-turn right in the middle of the road. I'm not expecting it, so I don't have my body set. I thought she was going to pull into a drive to turn around or something, but she didn't. Lynn's kind of a daredevil.

"Whoa!" I say, my hands reaching out to grab the door, the dashboard, to steady myself. She laughs like I'm a comedian, and I laugh too.

We ride for a while with the wind blasting our faces. The sun is setting, streaking the sky between the trees with dusky gold and tangerine, and it's beautiful. I don't know what is better, watching the sunset through the windshield or the reflection of it dancing across Lynn's sunglasses. It's one of those moments where I want the world to stop, time to hold still, so I can just take my time and savor it. Because magical moments like this, they don't happen that often. I catch my breath, like maybe that will make it pause, but it doesn't work. Time keeps barreling forward. Lynn makes a left and the sunset is to the side of us now, lost behind a thick bank of trees.

Chapter Three

Dairy Queen is a bit of a letdown. Nobody we know is there. Nobody to watch us arrive in Lynn's car. No one oohing and ahhing with envy. I don't piss and moan about it though. Don't want her to remember whose idea it was. Instead I act like I really had a craving for ice cream and splurge on a Pecan Mudslide. Then it's Lynn's turn to order, but instead of getting some kind of ice-cream thing like she usually does, she says, "I'll have a coffee, please."

Coffee? I look at her to see if she's joking, but she doesn't appear to be. Since when does Lynn drink coffee?

And then I see the way she's smiling at the guy at the till, and the whole "coffee" thing starts making sense. It's some guy who graduated from our school last year. He's got that whole casually tossed, carefully styled, highlighted hair thing going on, a tiny silver lightning bolt pierced through his earlobe, a poet's patch lurking under his lower lip. He was one of the hotshots of the graduating class. What was his name? I can't remember. I think it was Chazz or something like that. I'm kind of surprised to see him working here. I would have thought he'd be at university somewhere, on a sports scholarship or something.

Now, normally this kind of guy wouldn't give us the time of day. He'd never even glance in our direction. But he must see what I noticed in Lynn on the car ride over, because he's looking at her like he's a hungry dog.

"One Pecan Mudslide," he says. And even though it's my purchase he's sliding across the counter, I could just as well be the soft-ice-cream machine. "And…" He does a drumroll. "Coffee for the lovely lady." He winks at Lynn. How cheesy is that? Who the hell winks in this day and age?

"Come on," I say, grabbing my ice cream. "Let's sit over here." I think she's following me, but when I plop down in my seat, I can see that the guy is still chatting her up. He's giving her a pen, a napkin, and now she's writing her name and phone number down. This guy is way too old for her, but there's nothing I can do about it. So I eat my ice cream and pretend like I'm enjoying it.

When Lynn finally makes her way to our table, it's like she's only half there. Her body is with me, sipping nasty, bitter coffee, but her mind, her smile—they're still hanging out with Chad. Apparently that's his name, Chad. Sheesh, even his name reeks of corn.

Chapter Four

"He hasn't called yet," Lynn says, spinning her combination lock back around, landing on 32.

"Well…" I'm pretending like I don't understand it either, but really, I don't know what Lynn's been smoking. This guy's not going to call some starry-eyed eleventh grader no matter how cute she is. "It's only been two days," I say. "Maybe he lost it or something."

She jerks hard on her lock and it opens with a snick. "I doubt it." Lynn slams her books in her locker and takes out her lunch. "He probably came to his senses. Why would he want to date me? He probably thinks I'm a loser."

"Isn't that a little extreme? Maybe he's busy. Maybe he already has a girl-friend."

"Then why," Lynn says patiently, like I'm really stupid, "would he ask for my number?"

"Because he's an asshole?" I say helpfully.

"Oh, shut up." She whacks me on the arm. Not hard. Not in a mean way.

"Maybe he likes collecting phone numbers so he can feel like a hotshot. Relive his glory days."

"Give me a break. Chad wouldn't do that."

"How do you know?"

"I just know. The guy's perfect." No way to argue with that kind of logic, so I keep my mouth shut while Lynn closes her locker. We swing by the bathroom so she can give her hair a brush, reapply her strawberry lip-gloss. I put some on too, and then we head out to the field.

I think she's going to let the subject drop, but I'm no more than two bites into my tuna fish sandwich when she starts up again.

"Do you think he's going to call?"

"Who?"

"Chad," Lynn says impatiently.

It's really a no-win situation. "I don't know," I say. "What about Dwayne? I thought you were going out with him."

"Oh puleaze!"

"What? I thought you were."

"I'm done with him," Lynn snorts in disgust. "He's too young. So babyish!"

"But…" I say, feeling slightly panicky. "He's our age."

"So what. He doesn't act like it. Last weekend we went for a hike."

"Um-hmm…" I nod. I don't know what's so wrong with going for a hike.

"Well, I packed a nice picnic lunch, brought a blanket. I even bribed my brother to buy me a bottle of Baby Duck."

She shakes her head. Bites into her carrot angrily.

"I went through all that trouble to make it nice and romantic. But does he *do* anything? No! I even pretended to fall asleep when he was feeling me up for Christ's sake! So he wouldn't feel shy about trying to go further. I mean, what more does he want?"

Lynn throws her hands up in disgust. "No. I'm done with Dwayne. We've been going out for six months now, and the most he ever wants to do is kiss and touch my breasts. And it takes at least an hour for him to work up the courage to do that!"

It's funny how she's mad about Dwayne being so shy and respectful of her.

There is a cheer at the end of the field. Some of the guys are playing soccer. Ricky is running around pumping his fists in the air. He must have scored.

"I wonder what it's like," Lynn says after a long pause.

"What what's like? Soccer?" It's kind of hard to follow her.

"No. You know. What *it's* like. Doing it. I want to know." There's such longing in her voice. Such curiosity. I can't imagine what it's like to be her.

She turns to face me. "What do you think it looks like?"

My face flushes. An image flashes into my head, but she can't possibly be talking about that. We never talk as frankly as that.

"What?" My voice squeaks a bit.

"You know, their thing," she says, laughing at the expression on my face. "Have you ever seen one?"

"No!" I say, even though I have. I've seen Larry's. It happened last week. He'd accidentally left the bathroom door open. I guess he was getting ready to take a piss. Maybe he thought I'd already left for school. I don't know. Anyway, I walked by.

"Oops," he'd said, turning to give me the full-on view. He was dressed for work, suit, tie, polished black shoes, matching belt, and then there was his penis, all mottled and limp, lying in his hand.

"Haley," he'd said, smiling slightly, as if I'd walked by on purpose to take a peek. I turned away quickly, cheeks flaming, and walked away. I thought I heard him laugh, but I'm not sure. It might have been the back screen door slamming behind me.

I want to tell Lynn it's not so great, seeing one. It's not so special. Kind of disgusting if you want to know the truth, but how do I tell her that? What would she think? That I was spying on my mom's new boyfriend taking a pee?

"I wonder what it looks like." Lynn interrupts my thoughts.

"I don't know," I say.

"I wonder what it looks like hard."

There is another cheer at the end of the field.

"Oh look," I say, jumping to my feet. "Somebody scored again." I pretend to watch for a couple of seconds and then say, "Hey, you want to go for a walk? I want to get a drink from the cafeteria."

Lynn starts laughing. "Oh, Haley, you are such an innocent." Like she's oh-so-sophisticated.

"I am not," I say, turning away from her, heading for the school. By the time she catches up with me, my face is back to its normal color.

Chapter Five

It's colder today. There was frost on the train tracks this morning as I was walking to school. It made them kind of slippery. But does the cold deter Lynn? No, she wants ice cream. Not just any ice cream. It was decided at lunch that we were going to go to Dairy Queen after school. And don't get me wrong, I'm glad I don't have to walk home today...but Dairy Queen again?

"Lynn," I say, as we make our way through the hordes of fleeing students. "You know, I was thinking, maybe we should…" We emerge through the back doors of the school, the sunlight bright in our eyes. "…go somewhere else. He's not going to be there."

"How do you know?" Lynn says, cutting across the pathetic strip of lawn.

"He hasn't been there the last five times we've gone."

"We've just got to figure out what his hours are. What days he works."

"But why?" I'm getting impatient with her. "I mean, really, if he wanted to get in touch with you, he would have called. Not to mention, I'm getting pretty sick of ice…"

"Hey!" someone shouts. "Watch out." I leap to the side. Thank God I have good reflexes because I barely avoid a head-on collision with that pain in the ass, Justin. He's trying to impress his stupid gaggle of groupies, that follows him around the school, by doing wobbly figure eights on his unicycle.

"*You* watch out!" I snap. I mean, God. Give me a break. I run to catch up with Lynn, who has already reached the edge of the parking lot. But that isn't a good move because I almost smack into the back of her. Not my fault, of course. She was walking regular speed when all of a sudden she stopped dead in her tracks.

"Haley," she says in a half whisper, clutching my arm. "He's here! Oh my god, he's here at our school!"

It doesn't take a brain surgeon to figure out who she's talking about. There's Chad, with a group of guys, admiring someone's chromed-out motorcycle. But even worse, Chad's butt is resting up against the passenger side of Lynn's car.

"It's fate," Lynn breathes. "This is my chance. How do I look?"

"You look great," I say, even though I don't have a good feeling in my stomach. What's this guy doing at our school? He graduated. Why's he hanging around in our parking lot with a bunch of twelfth graders?

Lynn digs around in her purse for her car keys, her good-luck talisman. "Here they are," she says, scooping them out, casually twirling them on her forefinger. She's obviously been practicing this move a lot. She's got it down good.

"Let's go," she says, and we head toward her car. "So, Haley, where do you want to go?" Lynn asks nonchalantly, in a slightly louder voice than normal.

I'm not quite sure how I'm supposed to answer this one. Is it a real question? Am I supposed to tell the truth? Or lie and say Dairy Queen?

"How about Dairy Queen?" I'm speaking a little louder than normal too. I don't want to, but I am her friend. "I could do with a Dilly Bar."

"Nah." Lynn tosses her head. "I don't feel like Dairy Queen today. How about Starbucks?" Starbucks my ass!

"Sure," I say. "Starbucks sounds good."

"Excuse me," Lynn says to Chad, nudging him with her elbow. "But she has to get in here." Like I'm a two-year-old and can't speak for myself.

Chad looks up. Obviously I don't register. Lynn doesn't either, until she does that swirl thing with her keys on her forefinger, and his eyes follow the swing of the car keys around to her face. I can see him trying to put the pieces together. Pulling her face up from the doubtless hundreds of girls that he has logged into his brain.

"I know you," he says, catching her finger, her keys in their mid-circle swirl. Their eyes catch too. "Where was it?" he says.

Lynn smiles, bites her lower lip slightly, releases it. "I don't know," she says, sounding truly perplexed. I had no idea she was such a good actress.

"Thetis Lake maybe…this summer?"

"No…I don't think so." She shakes her head like she's confused.

"Andrew's party last weekend?"

"Um…"

"Dairy Queen," I say, cutting through the bull. "You met her at Dairy Queen."

I'm surprised at how loud my voice sounds. Loud and flat.

"You think?" Lynn says, looking dubious.

"That's right," Chad says. "No, she's right. That's where I remember you from, Dairy Queen. You came in, what, a couple of weeks ago."

"I did?"

"Yeah, you gave me your number."

"Oh…Oh yeah." Lynn smiles. "I remember now. You look different in your regular clothes."

"Yeah, that uniform is pretty bad."

"Yeah," Lynn says, laughing with him. "Poor you. Oh well, it's a job."

"Was a job," Chad says, smiling ruefully. "I got fired." I'm tempted to say, No wonder all our trips to Dairy Queen turned out a bust. But I don't. Instead I stand there smiling as if this is fun for me too.

"This your car? Or your parents'?" he says.

"It's mine." Lynn runs her hand along the roof. "All mine." And the way she says

"All mine," it's as if her words are dipped in honey, coming out all slow and sweet and full of promise.

"Cool," Chad leans forward, setting both his hands on either side of Lynn's shoulders, resting on her car. "You got your own wheels." He smiles at her like she's all that matters. "Wanna take me for a spin?"

"Absolutely," Lynn says, giving her hair a slow toss. Her eyes, a dare.

And that's it. He hops in the front passenger seat. Lynn gets behind the wheel, and she pulls out, tires spitting gravel and dust.

"Guess you aren't going to Starbucks," one of his friends says with a smirk.

"Oh, shut up." I don't even look at him, just fling the words over my shoulder as I start the long walk home.

Chapter Six

Mom pokes at the gloop in her bowl. "How on earth did you manage to burn the chili? That's like burning soup, for crying out loud."

"Your girl has real talent," Larry says. They are both laughing, like I'm such a funny little girl. And it pisses me off, how they're being so condescending.

"If you don't like it, then why are you eating it?" I mutter under my breath.

"Haley." Mom sounds shocked. "Don't be rude."

Rude? *I'm* being rude? I'm supposed to sit here and suck it up? Them talking about me like I'm not even here? Like I'm a two-year-old or something? I'm supposed to be polite to this donkey's ass just because she likes him? And the memory of seeing his dick lying in his hand, the expression on his face, makes something in me snap. The next thing I know I'm standing up.

"Look," I shout, slamming my hands on the table, "I didn't *mean* to burn it, okay! It's not like I did it on purpose. It's not like I said, *Oh*, I'm going to go through all this trouble of making a nice dinner for every-body and then I'm going to burn it because *that* will be fun! Jeeze, Mom, what do you think I am? Some kind of idiot?"

"Haley!" Mom says, her eyes flashing daggers. "That's *enough*." Like Larry's feelings are more important than mine.

"You're right. It's enough!" I'm crying now too, which really surprises me. I mean, it's only stupid chili for God's sake. But it's like someone is taking over my body, and I can hear my voice scream, "I've had it. I've had it up to here! I'm done. Make your own damn dinner from now on."

Mom might be answering now, but if she is, I can't hear. Whatever. I storm out of the kitchen, and when I get to my bedroom, I slam the door hard. Grab my calculus book off the bed and hurl it at the door. It makes a satisfying thunk.

"Stupid bitch!" I say, which feels good, but it's a mixed sort of good. It's freeing, sort of, to use that word about my mom. But I'd be lying if I didn't say that it makes me feel guilty too. Even though she deserves it.

Chapter Seven

Mom didn't come up. She always comes to my room after we fight. Always. We talk and sort it out and apologize. And we don't just talk about the fight and what happened and what was said. We talk about everything, life, what's going on at school, me and Lynn, her friends at work. We always do this. I don't understand why she didn't come up. It's not like I called her a stupid bitch to her face. I said it behind her back, and quietly too. There's no way she ever could have heard me.

I figured for sure she'd come up after Larry left. But she didn't. Just went into her bathroom, ran the water for a while, brushed her teeth, washed her face. I thought about going in there and telling her to turn off the taps because there is getting to be a real water crisis in the world. But she'd take it wrong. Anyway, it isn't up to me to make the first move. It was her fault, making that rude comment about my cooking and then letting Larry dis me as well.

I can't believe she hasn't come up. She has always had a rule about not going to sleep angry. Sometimes I've thought it was a stupid rule, but now I'm used to it.

And while I was sitting in my room, waiting for the sound of her footsteps, I thought over what had happened at dinner. Mom and Larry were rude, but I over-reacted too. I wanted to tell her that. Maybe I'd even tell her about what happened with Lynn and Chad in the parking lot today.

How she drove off without me. Didn't even call me later to apologize or explain.

I want to tell Mom that I looked this Chad guy up in my old yearbook, and the whole thing doesn't make sense. He wasn't just *a* hotshot, he was *the* hotshot. He was Mister Everything. Which is fine on its own, but the thing that has me concerned is that in practically every picture of him, he's got his arm around a different girl. The guy's obviously a player. I want Mom's advice as to what I should do.

Maybe I'd even find a way to mention that Larry flashed me. It was probably an accident. But just in case, shouldn't she know? I don't know what to do. She really likes this guy. I don't want to cause trouble. Maybe I should let it go, put it out of my head, because there is no easy answer, and it hurts my stomach every time I think about it.

I wish it was the old days and I could talk with Mom the way we used to. But I can't. She was too busy with her sleazy boyfriend, and then she went to bed. Couldn't care less that I was upset.

I glance over at the clock. 1:47 the digital red numbers glow back at me. I'm never going to get to sleep. It doesn't matter how hard I try. My mind's leaping around like a gymnast on speed. I shake my thoughts away from Lynn, only to have them land on the argument with my mom. Shake them off my mom, and there's Larry's stupid face smirking at me. Life sucks. It really does.

Chapter Eight

It's raining. The cafeteria is jam-packed. Lynn and I are huddled at the end of a table, sharing a seat. The cafeteria generally smells, but on really rainy days, it's always worse. It's the combination of old wet sneakers, BO, the crush of bodies, the grease from the fryer, school lunches mixed with people brown-bagging it, pickles and stale peanut butter sandwiches on day-old bread.

There's such a crush of humanity in here. The windows are fogged up, droplets gather, swell and then burst and morph into tiny rivulets that trickle down.

"Chad is *amazing*! This guy is a god." Lynn hasn't stopped talking since we met at her locker. "I can't believe he was right there in the parking lot. Standing by my car. What are the odds of that?" I open my mouth to answer, but there's no need. "About one in a million," she prattles. "A billion even. And yet…there he was!"

She hugs herself happily. No "Sorry I ditched you, Haley. Sorry, I didn't call." It's like it didn't happen.

"And you know what I was thinking?" I don't even bother to open my mouth this time. "I was thinking that maybe… just maybe…he lost my phone number but remembered me from last year, and so he came by the school and hung around the parking lot in the hopes of maybe running into me."

She pauses to draw in a breath and I leap into the gap. Thanks to my yearbook perusal, I'm prepared. I have plenty of ammunition.

"Lynn, he wouldn't have remembered you from last year. He wouldn't have even noticed you."

"He might have," Lynn says, a trifle defensively.

Now, normally, I might let Lynn spin her fancy fairy tale, but I don't feel like it. Not after the way she ditched me in the parking lot. Besides, this guy's a player. So if you look at it that way, I'm actually being noble.

"Nope," I say cheerfully. "Wouldn't have given you the Kleenex he blew his nose on. Number one, he was the top scorer on the basketball team. The team that finally pulled itself together and actually made it to the B.C. championships. Number two, I don't know if you remember correctly, but he was still working his way through the female population of the senior class. Every once in a while he would indulge in an eleventh-grade girl, but he never got around to tenth."

"How do you know?"

"Come on, Lynn. Look in last year's yearbook. There's only a million pictures of him strutting around the school, his arm flung around a multitude of girls. And last but not least, we get to number three. The salient fact that, last year, you were not quite the girl that you are today."

"What do you mean?" Lynn asks angrily.

I know I'm being smug, but I can't help it. I figured this whole thing out last night. Funny the things that fall into place when you can't sleep. "Let's just say you've gone up a few bra sizes and you've lost the braces, not to mention you are the brand-new owner of a pretty nice car."

"Chad's not like that! He doesn't like me because of that. You're just jealous because he likes me better than you."

"I don't care whether Chad likes me or not. It's you that I'm worried about." But even as I say these words, I wonder if they're true. Why am I pissing on her parade?

Chapter Nine

I call Lynn as soon as I get home. "I'm sorry," I say. "I don't know what got into me. I know how much you wanted to see him again."

"It's okay," Lynn says.

"Oh good."

"But he does like me for me you know." Her words are sure, but I can hear the doubt in her voice, and I feel bad because I was the one who put it there.

"I'm sure he does," I say. "I was just mad because you ditched me after school."

"But it was Chad!"

"I know it was Chad. I understand. It felt a little funny is all, watching you drive off with him when we were planning to do something."

"But we were planning to try and find Chad. What would be the point of trying to track him down when…"

I finish the sentence for her. "He was standing right beside your car. I understand. It's just I felt like I suddenly became invisible or something. Like I didn't matter."

"You matter," Lynn says. "You're my best friend."

"Okay," I say, smiling into the phone. I'm relieved that we're having this conversation and sorting things out. "You want to do something?"

"Of course," Lynn says. "It's Friday night, isn't it? Shall we go to the rink?"

"Sounds good. I'll meet you out front, six forty-five."

"No, I'll pick you up." Lynn's laughing.

I start laughing too. "Oh yeah, I forgot, you've got a car! That's so cool."

We get off the phone and I go upstairs to figure out what to wear. My outfit comes together pretty easily, quicker than I'd thought. Which is kind of nice for a change. I've got music playing, good and loud, plenty of time for my makeup.

On my way to the bathroom, my foot bangs into my old Christmas stocking, which is still half-stuffed with things I haven't gotten around to using yet. But instead of a bar of lavender soap or a still-wrapped toothbrush, a tube of glittery body lotion shoots out.

I'm kind of surprised. I don't remember seeing that when I opened my stocking. It seems like a sign or something, so I open it up and rub a little bit on my arms and on the exposed part of my chest. It smells pretty. Looks nice too. Gives me a little bit of shimmer and shine. It'll look good at the rink under those fancy lights they have going for Teen Skate. I especially like how the Couples Only skate portion looks. Not only do they have the special lights on, but they dim all the lights as well. It's really romantic.

Just thinking about it makes my belly race slightly. Maybe a cute guy will ask me to skate. "You never know," I say to the mirror.

I try to smile that mysterious, come-hither sexy smile the models in the hair and makeup commercials do. You know, that sort of half smile they have. I think it looks a little better than the one I do when I'm not thinking about it. My natural one is all teeth. There's nothing about my regular smile that would make anyone say, "Who is that girl?" I've been practicing a little bit. Not sure if I have it down right, though.

I apply a little blush, a brush of eye shadow, a dab of mascara, some lip-gloss. I brush my hair until it's gleaming. Then I practice my smile one last time and give my hair a Charlie's Angels toss.

That's when my cell phone rings. It startles me. I almost don't answer it for a second. I don't know why. I just stare at it ringing on my counter. It's got to be Lynn. She's probably calling because she got here early and is out in front of my house. My phone rings again. I grab it quick before it diverts her to my message box.

"Hello?" I say, slightly breathless.

"Hey, Haley," Lynn says, super cheerfully, which immediately makes me suspicious. "What are you doing?" she chirps.

"What do you think I'm doing? I'm getting ready. Actually, I'm pretty much ready right now. Where are you? Are you here already?" I ask even though I'm pretty sure she's not. I can feel it in my gut.

There's a pause on the other end of the line.

"Um..." Lynn says. "Haley?" She's using that hesitant little-girl voice that might work on mothers and boys, but it definitely doesn't work on me.

"Please don't tell me you're flaking out on me," I say.

"It's just..." She's talking over me now, her words rushing out. "Chad called, and he wants me to go to a party with him. I mean, this is the first time he's asked me out. Like to go somewhere..."

"You and Chad drove all over town yesterday after school."

"But that doesn't count!" Lynn interrupts. "Not really. That wasn't like a date or anything. It just happened."

"Well, what did you tell him?" Lynn doesn't answer. "Did you tell him we already have plans?"

I hear Lynn clear her throat. "Not... exactly."

"What did you say?" I already know. I want Lynn to have to say it out loud. Be truthful about the fact that this is the second day in a row that she's blown me off for Chad.

"I said that I'd go to the party with him." There is a silence now. Because really, there's not much else to say. I wait for a second or two more, in case Lynn decides that it would probably be nice if she invited me to go to the party with them. Since it is a party and not a date-date, like dinner for two. But she doesn't. She just says, in an I'm-so-miserable-this-is-such-a-hard-choice voice, "I'm so sorry, Haley. I really like this guy, and it might be the only time he asks me out."

"Whatever," I say and hang up the phone. I catch my reflection in the mirror, all dressed up and nowhere to go. "Great. This is just great."

I stomp out of the bathroom, flop on my bed. I wish I was a little kid again so I could bang my heels on the wall, over and over, wail my head off, until my mom came upstairs to see what was the matter. And then, after she'd comforted me, we'd go downstairs and make a big batch of sugar cookies. We'd use the heart-shaped cookie cutter, and she'd let me be in charge of sprinkling the red sugar crystals on the top. I miss those days. When everything was simple. Thinking about it fills me with this odd sort of longing.

There's a knock at my bedroom door. "Come in," I say, half sitting up. Maybe Mom and I can go to the movies or something.

The door swings open, but it's not Mom who steps inside. It's Larry. He shuts the door behind him. My stomach drops.

"Haley...Haley...Haley," he says.

I feel scared. Don't know why. "What are you doing in my room?"

He doesn't answer.

"Could you please get out of my room," I say. I'm trying to sound polite, like this isn't sort of freaking me out. "I'd like some privacy, please."

He doesn't leave.

"Where's Mom? Mom!" I call. No answer.

He laughs, soft under his breath. "She can't hear you. She went to the liquor store to pick up some Limoncella. I'm going to treat her to my famous lemon-drop martini. Maybe we'll even let you have one." He smiles. "If you behave." He pushes away from the doorframe. "Nope, it's just you and me, babe," he says, sauntering toward me on the bed. "And you are looking real good."

I get up off the bed two times in my head before my legs actually move me. I try to make it around him, but my feet slip, get tangled up in all the crap on my floor. It's not enough to make me fall, but it's that skid, that extra second of hesitation, that is my undoing. Suddenly, I'm falling to the floor. Falling, or was I pushed? I hit the ground hard. His body lands on mine. I try to get up, but I can't get him off me. His body's too heavy. Squashing me down. Can't breathe.

"Get off!" I push at him hard, with both hands. The next thing I know, he's pinned my hands over my head. I'm stunned how fast this guy can move.

"It seems that we've fallen," he says, like he's talking about the color of his necktie.

"Get *off*." I can't get free, no matter how hard I twist and turn.

"Hold still. Let me help you. You're all tangled up in this stuff on the floor." That's what he says, but his hand is sliding under my top, pushing it up. I squeeze my eyes shut, trying not to cry. But I know what he's doing. I can feel the cold air on my stomach first and then my breasts.

"Stop...*please* don't!" But he's touching them now, and I can't get away.

"Oh yeah...You like that, don't you."

"No, I *don't*."

"Yes, you do. I hate to correct you, my dear, but you're really quite wrong about that. I've never seen somebody so hot for me. But that's okay. I'm a great believer in education."

I try to twist my body out from under him, get away.

"Hold still, you bitch," he says, his voice suddenly harsh. And it's almost like I hear it before I feel it, his hand making contact with my face. My eyes fly open from the force of the impact.

But I don't look at him. Anywhere but at him. I will not cry. I won't give him the satisfaction. "You're hot for me. You want me. It's really quite disgusting, you coveting your mother's boyfriend. But the truth is there." His voice switches again, soft and reasonable. "I'm always one to support the truth." He kisses me on the forehead. I feel his hand start to slide down.

"*Don't!* Please, *please* don't." But his hand keeps moving. It's working with the button on my jeans now.

"I don't imagine," he says, his mouth on my breast, tongue circling, "that your mother would be too pleased. You, carrying on with her boyfriend this way, right under her nose. Inviting him into your room. All sprawled out on the bed the way you were. An open invitation."

"I didn't…invite you in!" It's too late. I'm crying now, can't help it.

"Oh yes you did, my dear. Never argue with a lawyer. I knocked. You said, Come in. Your words precisely. You invited me in."

He manages to get the top button of my pants open, starts working on the zipper.

"Get off! Get off of me." But I can't move him. His hand is in my pants now, sliding down. "Get off!"

He's almost touching me there when the kitchen door slams and we hear my mom calling out.

"I got Limoncella, Larry."

"Damn," he says. His hand stills.

"Larry?"

Suddenly both his hands are wrapped around my neck, tight. Can't breathe.

"I should probably kill you," he whispers, mouth up close to my ear. "Do your mother a favor. She's a nice woman. Good and decent. She doesn't deserve to have a slut like you for a daughter. It's not fair. It would break her heart if she knew about you."

I'm scared I'm going to die. No air coming in, my face is going to explode, my lips and eyeballs are pulsing.

"Tell you what. You promise to behave, no more coming on to me, and I won't have to kill you. Okay? Nod yes if you can agree to what I am saying."

My vision is blacking out around the edges. I manage to nod my head. I don't know how, his hands are clenching my throat so tight. My vision is only the size of a tennis ball now.

Suddenly he releases me. The hands around my neck are gone. I feel him pinch my nipple, roll it around in his fingers. I don't even bother to swipe his hand away. I just lie there. "Good girl," he says. He stands up over me, adjusts himself, smooths his hands over his hair. "I'm glad we understand each other," he says, and then he's gone.

Chapter Ten

By the time I get to the rink, Teen Skate is almost half over. Normally, I wouldn't bother, because the cost is the same no matter what time you arrive. But I needed to go somewhere. Get out of the house.

I pay my money, go inside and get some skates. The guy behind the counter gives me a pretty beat-up pair. I doubt there will be much ankle support in them, but at least they are sharp. I lace up.

It takes me a bit longer than usual because my hands are still shaking. Actually everything is. It started right after Larry walked back downstairs. I would have thought the shakes would have passed by now. It's not too noticeable though.

When I get my skates laced up, I walk stiff-legged over to the rink. I try to look normal, like nothing just happened on my bedroom floor with Larry. I'm just a regular kid, like everybody else, out for Friday night fun. I try to pretend that I don't notice I'm alone. That Lynn's not with me. Act like I couldn't care less.

Nobody should be able to tell what happened to me. I washed my face, reapplied my makeup. I wanted to take a shower, wash the memory of him off me, but I needed to get out of the house even more.

I step onto the ice. Push off. Start skating. Focus on that. I'm an okay skater. Not good, not bad, just okay. At least I don't fall down all the time or have to cling to the side. I can skate forward and backward a little bit. Not like the guys who play hockey. They can skate backward just as fast as forward and can stop on a dime. I can slow down to a stop, but I can't do that abrupt sideways stop that sends ice flecks flying.

My legs are burning, and I've only circled the arena three times. My throat's ragged, like someone's been scraping hard on the inside with a scrub brush. I feel like his hands are still circled around my throat. His words in my ears, how I asked for it. Invited him in.

I try not to think about my mom. She would be upset, no doubt about it. She really likes him a lot. His word against mine. I wonder who she would believe. Her daughter? Or her boyfriend, a high-flying lawyer, a partner in Hamlin, Smith and Company? A man whose job is all about interpreting the law. And the problem is, I did invite him in. I thought he was my mom, but I have no way to prove that. I can't believe how things got so mixed up. I mean, he thought I was coming on to him! That's crazy. Why would I do that?

A guy from my math class whizzes by, body low, arms swinging, long smooth strides. It's funny. He's so quiet and shy in class, you'd never know he was such a good skater. I try to lengthen my stride a bit, make it less choppy.

My eyes feel funny. Like they're still sort of bulging. When he was choking me, I was scared my eyes were going to shoot right out of my head, like stomped-on grapes. I don't know if eyes can do that or not, but I tell you, have somebody wrap their hands around your neck tight and you'll see what I mean. I hate that guy. I don't know how he could have misunderstood me so badly. I definitely wasn't inviting him in. I thought he was my mom.

"Hey, Haley."

I look over. Michelle and Audrey are skating beside me. I don't know how long they've been there. Did they just arrive? Or have they been watching me for a while? If so, did my face give any of my thoughts away?

"Hey," I say with a big smile. "Hi, guys."

"Where's Lynn?" Michelle asks.

"Oh," I say, rolling my eyes, "she's out with Chad."

"Chad? Not Chad Skylander?" Audrey squeals. "Oh my god, he's so hot!"

"Yeah," I say, with a little laugh. "That's just what Lynn said." I'm really surprised at how conversational and normal my voice sounds. It's like Lynn didn't ditch me, and I didn't almost get strangled on my bedroom floor. I'm just skating around the rink like I'm some happy-go-lucky feature in *Seventeen* magazine.

"She's so lucky," Michelle says wistfully. "I bet now you guys will get invited to all the really hot parties and everything."

"Maybe," I say. I don't tell them that's where Lynn is right now. At a hot party, and I wasn't invited. I just act like, yeah, probably there will be tons of parties, and maybe I'll go, and maybe I won't. Depends on my mood.

"Lucky," Michelle says again.

"Yeah," Audrey says. Not much I can say to that, so I just smile and nod, like, yeah, life is so great. They skate off, and I'm back to skating around the rink by myself.

Normally, after skating this many times around, Lynn and I would go get a hot chocolate or go to the bathroom to brush our hair and reapply lip-gloss, hoping to bump into some cute guys. But I'm by myself, and it's totally different. So even though my legs are tired, I keep on skating.

Chapter Eleven

I take my time unlacing the skates and handing them in, getting my shoes. It always feels odd to walk after skating. It's almost like I have to remember how. Everything feels sort of floppy.

I'm one of the last people to leave. I take my time walking home. I hope Larry's gone. That mom's not having him sleep over tonight. It's pretty dark. There's not much of a moon out tonight, and it keeps getting covered up by clouds. There are a lot of cars though, casting off light, headlights arcing across the road, and then red glowing tail lights disappearing in the distance. Every once in a while one comes along, music blasting, and I scrunch down in my jacket. Hope it's not Lynn. I don't want her to see me walking home all alone, like some pathetic friendless loser.

Another car speeds by. Someone flings a beer can out the back window. I jump back, but it really wasn't necessary. The guy had bad aim. It missed me by a mile. "Screw you!" I yell, giving them the finger. Doesn't really help things, but makes me feel better. Probably not the smartest thing to antagonize a carload of drunken red-necks. I'm glad to see their car doesn't slow down, but just keeps on going, disappearing over the crest of the hill.

I'm halfway up our drive before I realize I'm holding my breath. I let it out. Try to calm my body. I hope Larry's not here. Maybe they went over to his house, or out or something.

I come around the back of the house and there is his black Jaguar sitting in the drive. My first impulse is to hide. Which I realize, sitting here behind mom's purple flowering rhododendron bush, is really stupid. It's his car for Christ's sake. He's not even in it. What's it going to do? Run me over driverless like in some kind of cheesy horror movie?

Maybe Lynn's back from the party and I could sleep over at her house. I call her cell phone. The ground is damp on my butt. Either she's not picking up or her batteries are dead. I don't bother leaving a message. I call her home phone. It rings four times. I'm just about to hang up when Lynn's mom answers.

"Hello?" She sounds really sleepy. I think I woke her up.

"Um…Hello, Mrs. Masterson, I'm so sorry to bother you. Is Lynn there?"

"I don't think she's home yet, honey. Do you want me to go check her bedroom?"

"Would you mind?"

"No problem, sweetie." She always does that. Calls me "sweetie" and "honey." I don't mind though. It makes me feel like she thinks of me as family.

She comes back to the phone. "No, Lynn's not back yet. Shouldn't be long." Lynn's mom stifles a yawn. For a second I'm tempted to ask if I can sleep over anyway. But that might seem weird, so I don't.

"All right," I say, my voice, cheerful. "Thank you for checking. Sorry if I woke you."

"Don't worry," she says. "I'll go right back to sleep. No problem." I hear her yawn again as the phone hangs up.

Damn. Now what? I can't stay hanging out in the bushes all night. I wish I had somewhere to go. I've got to make more friends. One is not enough.

I decide to check out the house. I stay in the shadows, avoid the porch light. If I can figure out where they are, maybe I can get in without being seen. Hopefully they are in Mom's bedroom. That would make things easy.

I circle around to the side. The living room lights are still on. But maybe they forgot to turn them off. I can't see into the room from this angle, only the top part of the wall, some crown molding and the ceiling. I think about sneaking into the neighbors' yard and climbing their Garry oak, but then I see a shadow drift across the ceiling. They're in the living room. I'm having the worst luck today.

I try Lynn's cell phone again. She's still not picking up. I can't sleep out here. Besides, that would be stupid. Larry's not going away. They generally spend the weekends together and a couple of weeknights as well. So I better get it over with.

I mean, sure, the whole thing in my bedroom was really creepy. A case of mixed-up signals, that's for sure. But he made me promise to stop coming on to him, and I did. So that means that he knows I'm not going to be trying to seduce him, so he won't misread the signals and think that I am. Hopefully the whole thing was a big misunderstanding and it will never happen again. I mean, that's what we both want, right? So I'm probably making a big thing out of nothing. Freezing my ass off out here. It's pathetic that I'm scared to go inside. I head toward the house.

I shut the door behind me quietly. It's stupid that my heart is pounding so hard. I slip off my shoes, place them gently in the shoe bin by the door. I straighten and walk through the kitchen into the hall. I walk quietly, my feet making only the faintest, muted "shush" noise on the floor. I keep my eyes facing forward. I don't even glance toward the living room.

I'm almost past the doorway when I hear my mom call out. "Hello, Haley." I freeze. "We're having a little party in here," Mom says. "Want to join us?"

"Um…" I say. "I'm a little tired. I think I'm going to go to bed."

"We're having lemon-drop martinis." He's talking now. "What do you think?" he says to my mom. "We could make her a baby one." And there's something about the way he says this, the way the words roll off his tongue that makes me feel all dirty, and I know he's remembering, just like I am, what happened upstairs earlier tonight.

"I don't see why not," Mom says gaily. I pry my eyes off the floor and sneak a glance at her. She looks so happy. Her cheeks all flushed, like she believes in Prince Charming and happy-ever-after. "She's sixteen after all."

"She sure is," Larry says. "Legal age for a lot of things. Not booze, but a lot of other stuff. One martini won't hurt."

He steps into my view, slipping his arm around my mom's waist. "And I won't tell if you won't," he says, a little smile wrapping around his mouth.

My mom thinks he's talking to her. He's standing behind her and she can't see his face. But I can. He's pretending to talk to her, but we both know he's talking to me.

Mom laughs, bats him playfully with her hand. "That's so silly, Larry. Who am I going to tell? You're so funny!"

"It's okay," I say quickly. "I'm really tired. I'm going to bed." I don't wait for an answer, leave quickly. Head upstairs before they can stop me and insist that I stay. I lock the bedroom door behind me. As I do it, I feel this wave of sadness, like I'm shutting my childhood out. It's over and I can never go back.

Chapter Twelve

At first I thought it was part of my dream, the rap-tap sound, but then I realize someone is knocking on my door. Let me put it this way: after what happened yesterday, it was not a slow peaceful wake-up. I went from dead asleep to hyper-alert in two seconds flat.

"What? Who is it? What do you want?" I'm sitting upright. How I got in this position, I have no idea. I've got my comforter clutched up around my neck. Which is really overkill. First of all, the door is locked. Secondly, I'm wearing head-to-toe flannel pajamas. I'm totally covered.

"Haley." It's Mom. "Breakfast is almost ready, can you…" I see the door handle move, rattle. "Why is this door locked?" I leap out of bed and unlock the door.

"It is?" I say, trying to look surprised. "Huh?"

My mom's looking at me way too closely. "Why do you have the door locked, honey?" Her eyes start combing the room.

I feel my face flush. Can she tell what happened with Larry? Should I tell her? What would I tell her? He'd probably just deny it and twist it around to make it look like it was my fault.

Mom goes over to my bookshelf. "What's this, Haley?" She gestures at my abalone shell. There is a half-burned cone of incense that Lynn gave me. What does this have to do with what happened with Larry?

"Incense?" I say. I'm kind of confused. It's pretty obvious what it is. Even my mom, as naive as she is, must know what incense looks like.

She looks at me hard, like her eyes can see right through me. "Why are you burning incense, Haley?" she says pointedly. "You never used to."

Huh? Why is she going on about incense? "Lynn gave it to me and I was curious what it smelled like."

She starts sniffing the air, like a blood-hound. "I don't think so, Haley." Mom's acting like she thinks I'm lying or something. "I wasn't born yesterday." Double huh? "I know why people burn incense."

"You do?"

"Yes. To cover up the smell of marijuana."

"Marijuana?" I try not to smile. Mom calls it marijuana.

"Pot, hashish," Mom says, waving her hand impatiently. "Whatever you young people call it nowadays. What you call it doesn't matter. I'm here to tell you that smoking marijuana is a real bad idea. It's a road to nowhere. People are lacing that stuff with crystal meth so that unsuspecting kids like you will get hooked! Don't you smirk at me! I read a huge article about it in the newspaper." She shakes a finger in my face. "You will not smoke any more marijuana. You will not be locking your door. Do you understand?"

"Mom, I'm not smoking p—"

Mom cuts me off, her hand flying out in front of her body as if she's a traffic cop. "Ah…That's enough, don't say any more. I am not a fool. I can see the signs for myself. There will be no marijuana smoking, young lady, and no locking your door." Her eyes soften slightly. "I love you so much, Haley, but I cannot, will not, stand by and let you smoke yourself into a brain-mushed stupor."

She tries to give me a one-armed hug, but I stiffen my shoulder and shrug her off. Smoking pot? Jesus Christ. That's why she thinks I locked my door? Puh-lease! I haven't tried pot yet, but if

I did, I certainly wouldn't be stupid enough to do it in my bedroom. God. How dumb does she think I am?

"I know you're mad at me right now," she continues. "But I love you. This is for your own good." She gives me a some-day-when-you're-grown-you'll-thank-me smile and heads for the door. "Now come downstairs and set the table. I'm making buttermilk waffles. Larry's making us some fresh-squeezed orange juice. Delicious. I sure love that man."

So much for having a heart-to-heart talk about Larry. Not only do I have to deal with her messed-up boyfriend, who she's totally infatuated with, but she thinks I'm a lying, sneaking, pot-smoking teenager as well. If she wouldn't believe me about something as small as smoking pot, there's no way she's going to believe me about Prince Charming. I'm well and totally screwed.

I don't linger over breakfast. Why would I? I refuse his fresh-squeezed orange juice, even though Mom gives me a look like I'm being rude.

"Are you sure?" he says, placing a glass full of the stuff in front of my plate. "Have you ever tried it? You might like it."

"I hate orange juice," I say, pushing it away. "Especially fresh-squeezed."

"Haley!" Mom's voice is sharp. But Larry laughs like I said something funny, which pisses me off even more.

I eat my waffle in record time. Excuse myself, rinse off my plate, stick it in the dishwasher and go back upstairs. I lock my door after me. Why the hell not? If she thinks I'm such a badass, I might as well be one. I wish I had some pot. I'd smoke it right here and now, in my bedroom. I wouldn't even light the incense to mask the smell. Let that burning-cow-manure smell waft right down into the kitchen, to mingle with their buttermilk waffles and fancy OJ. Let it wrap around their nostrils.

That would show her. Who asked her to date some sleazy creep? Not me, that's for sure.

I try Lynn's cell again. No luck. She's still got it switched off. I leave her a text message to call me as soon as she can. I clean my room for the first time this century. Not because I want to. I'm never going to be able to find what I need without having everything laid out on the floor in its special pile. It's inconvenient, having to clean it all up. But in case Larry really is a perv in a pinstripe suit, I'm not going to leave anything lying around on the floor anymore that can tangle my feet and land me flat on my back.

Chapter Thirteen

"Holy crap," Lynn exclaims, staggering back like I smacked her in the face with a wet fish. "What the hell happened?" She gazes around my room in shock.

"I cleaned it," I say with a shrug. "It's not a big deal."

"Not a big deal? Are you kidding me? You never clean your room!"

"Well, I did. So what? I was ready for a change." I wish she'd stop going on about it. It's making me uncomfortable.

"It looks freaky. God." Lynn starts laughing. "What about your piles? How are you going to find stuff?"

"I'll manage, okay? Just leave it." My voice is way grouchier than I want it to be. Lynn's looking at me like I've sprouted two heads. I don't know what's wrong with me. "I'm sorry," I say. "It's just…"

"No, I'm sorry," Lynn says. "It's great you cleaned your room. It smells way better in here."

"My room wasn't gross dirty! It was clean dirty, mostly just clothes." Why am I being so defensive? Not to mention, I did find some pretty yucky things under my piles of stuff. A few old, moldy, half-eaten sandwiches, a petrified orange. Seriously disgusting stuff.

"Fine. Whatever," Lynn says, like she's thinking of turning around and going back out the door.

"Sorry," I say again. Jesus, I'm going to spend my whole damn day apologizing. It's not her fault my life's gone down the toilet. "I must be getting my period," I say, even though I'm not. It's a good explanation and one she'd understand. Lynn turns into a real harpy when it's her time of the month. "Tell me about last night."

Lynn's face lights up like a birthday cake. "Last night was amazing! I'm telling you, I'm so into this guy. He's perfect, so gorgeous, and sexy. Oh my god, I can't even tell you the things we did to each other last night. I wouldn't want to damage your virgin ears."

"Are you kidding me? You guys made out?"

She laughs, happily. Does a twirl. "We did more than make out. We did everything but."

"Everything?"

"That's right," Lynn says, laughing again as she hugs herself and falls on my bed. "If you can imagine it…we did it."

"Lynn!" I'm shocked. Really I am. It was only their first date. Not to mention, Lynn talking about this stuff is making all these images appear in my head. Images of Lynn doing things that I'd rather not be privy to. But memories of Larry too, the smell of his aftershave, the weight of his body grinding into mine, his hands around my throat, and I feel dirty all over again.

"It was fantastic!" Lynn says. "I *really* like it. This guy…he is so amazing. When you get around to it, Haley, you're really gonna like sex."

"I don't think I will," I say. I try not to let on how shaky this conversation is making me.

"No," Lynn says emphatically. "Trust me. You will." She sits up, like some amazing thought just struck her. "Haley, I might be in love."

"That's ridiculous, Lynn. You don't even know the guy."

"I know him better than I did." She wiggles her eyebrows.

"I don't want to hear about it."

"Okay, well maybe not in love." She grins. "Maybe 'in *lust*' would be a better description. Yes, that's right. I'm in lust." She leaps off the bed, makes a fine lady face, extends her hand, her pinkie lifted up. "Hello, how nice to meet you. My name is Lynn Masterson, and this is my boyfriend, Chad. We are very much in lust." She falls over in a heap of laughter.

"Lynn," I say. "This is serious. Chad's moving way too fast."

"Not fast enough if you ask me," Lynn says gleefully. "I would have gone the whole way last night if he'd asked me."

"Oh my god. Lynn, you could get pregnant. This guy could have some serious STD's."

"I don't care. I don't care." She starts making a song out of it. Gets up and starts dancing around the room. "I wanna do it, I wanna do it, I wanna do it with *Chad*!" The Chad part is accompanied by a pelvis thrust. "I wanna do it, I wanna do it, I wanna do it with *Chad*!"

"Lynn!" I'm trying to be the voice of reason, but she's bubbling over. It's like she's drunk on excitement, and I can't help but be happy for her, even though I'm concerned. She grabs both of my hands and tries to pull me into the dance. I shake her off, but I'm laughing now too, watching Lynn sing, dance and pelvic thrust her way around the room.

"You need to get yourself some condoms," I say.

Chapter Fourteen

We are strolling down the aisles of Shoppers Drug Mart. We already have a bag of Lay's All-Dressed potato chips, some Clorets, and some kick-ass dark purple nail polish in our basket, but that's not why we're here. We browse the shampoo.

"Smell this," Lynn says, unscrewing the lid of Primrose Lavender shampoo for me to smell. I take a whiff.

"Umm…" I say, even though I can't smell anything because they have a plastic security seal over the top. "That's pretty."

"It's organic too," Lynn says, like that should be a big selling point. "You want it?"

I shake my head. I'm Lynn's friend, but I'm not about to spend $11.99 on some organic shampoo. We've got plenty of regular shampoo at home. Not only that, what if I hate the smell?

"Well, you have to buy something," Lynn whispers, leaning in close.

"I am," I say, keeping my voice low as well. "I've got the chips." I'm trying to act cool, but my face is beet red. It seemed like a good idea for us to get Lynn some condoms when we were laughing it up in my bedroom, but now that I'm in the store I'm having second thoughts.

"Something else," Lynn says, a slight sheen of sweat appearing on her forehead and around her nose. "We can't just buy chips, gum and condoms, for Christ's sake."

"Why not? Besides, you've got the nail polish. That will be a total of four things. It won't look weird."

"Like you would know," she says dismissively, as if I'm a little kid that doesn't know anything.

"Fine." I grab the shampoo and throw it in our basket. "Fine, I'll get the dumb shampoo, but you owe me."

"Thanks." She smiles and we continue on our way, oh so casually, up the aisle and down the next to where the condoms are hanging. This is our fourth pass down this aisle. I'm hoping Lynn has the courage this time to grab a box.

"Which ones?" she says, her head facing forward, not moving her lips.

"What do you mean?" My mouth and head are doing the same thing. "Just grab a box and let's get out of here."

"Ribbed? Lubricated? What's the difference? What brand should I get?" She's looking kind of panicky. We are almost level with the condom section now. Lynn doesn't slow down. Now we are passing the condom section.

"Lynn, pick up the condoms."

"No, forget it. Keep walking. I don't need them."

"Oh, for Christ's sake." I reach out a hand and snag a box, plop it in our basket.

"Wow. I can't believe you did that," Lynn says. I'm kind of surprised myself. "What kind did you get?" Our feet are moving faster now, our heads still facing forward.

"I don't know. I'm not about to look." I say it gruffly, but actually I feel kind of invigorated. Like we just switched roles and I'm the brave one now. I feel good—that is, until I hear a little snort, and then another.

I glance over at Lynn. She is having a hard time stifling a laugh. "Don't even think about it!" I say fiercely. It's embarrassing enough walking down the aisle with Lynn's condoms in my basket, but it will be a million times worse if everyone is looking at us because she's howling with laughter. She bites her lip and makes her face serious. I pray it will hold until we get out of the door.

We arrive at the cashier. I try to hand the basket off to Lynn, but she won't take it. I'm not about to get in a hot-potato match here in the store. It would only draw more attention to our purchases. But I swear to God, Lynn owes me one.

I unload the nail polish, the Clorets. I make sure I pick up the potato chips and the condoms at once and put them down on the counter with the chips on top of the condoms so nobody will see them.

It was a pretty good plan, but the cashier must think I was trying to get away without paying for them or something, because the minute the stuff hits her counter, she rifles through it, spreading it out for the world to see. Her mouth tightens slightly when she sees the condoms. Or maybe it doesn't and I just think it does.

There are a few other customers in the lineup behind us. I can feel them shifting, breathing down my neck. Where did they all come from? There was no one here when we got to the checkout. Why does everyone in the whole store need to buy something right at this very moment?

"Nineteen dollars, twenty-eight cents," the cashier says.

"Give me some money," I say to Lynn, holding out my hand.

"No way," she says in a loud voice, taking a step backward. "Why should I pay for your stuff?" Lynn's eyes are twinkling. "I mean, I don't mind buying you a bag of chips every now and then, but *condoms*?"

I hear somebody snicker behind me.

"You're dead, Lynn," I hiss as I pay the cashier. "I can't *believe* you."

But she has already bolted out the door, and I can see her through the glass. She is supporting herself against the brick building, clutching the wall so she won't fall down. I can hear her pealing laughter through the shut door. Everybody in the store is looking at me. I am sure of it. I don't even bother glancing around. I collect my change, grab Lynn's bag of stuff and stomp out the door, ready to let her have it. But when she sees me, she peels herself off the building, still laughing, wiping the tears from her eyes.

"I love you, Haley," she says, face glowing. She gives me a big hug, and all my madness melts away. "You're the best!" She tucks her arm into mine and we walk down the street like that. Two friends, arm in arm, with a bagful of snacks and condoms, the late afternoon sun warming our faces.

Chapter Fifteen

"Steak?" Larry says, spearing one off the barbecue and holding it out.

It looks good, the juices dripping off it. My mouth is watering, but I don't answer. I walk right past and help myself to some of Mom's potato salad. I see him shrug out of the corner of my eye.

He turns his attention to Lynn, gives her his charming man smile. She smiles back as he plops my steak on her plate. I get this sinking feeling in my stomach. She doesn't know what he is. He says something to her. I can't hear what it is, but it makes her laugh. He laughs too, white teeth showing. He's got his shirt-sleeves rolled up, his gold watch catching the last slanting rays of sun.

My mom comes outside with a pitcher of fresh lemonade, the ice cubes clinking. He pulls her in for a hug. The expression on Mom's face is a sort of dreamy happiness as she snuggles into his chest, shuts her eyes with a soft sigh.

Seeing her like that sends a sharp pain to my heart. I've been thinking about it, and even if Larry thought I was coming on to him, he still shouldn't have pounced. He's with my mom! Even if I had been dancing around naked, which I wasn't, he shouldn't have tried to do anything. They are in a relationship. I shouldn't even be a temptation. He should want to stay faithful to her. So if he would try to get into my pants, with the slightest provocation, what's he doing to the rest of the world? I wish I knew what to do.

We sit down at the table. I make sure I sit down last so I won't end up next to him. Everybody digs in.

"Um…so good!" Mom says, cutting off a juicy, succulent bite of steak and popping it into her mouth. "You make the best barbecue, Larry."

"It is good," Lynn agrees. It smells delicious. I try to close my nostrils off.

Mom glances at my plate. She frowns. "Are you feeling okay?"

"Sure," I say, scooping up another mouthful of potato salad and washing it down with a slug of lemonade.

"Why don't you have a steak?"

"I don't feel like it," I say. I can feel Larry's eyes on me, but I don't glance over in his direction.

"You don't feel like steak?" Mom says incredulously. "Since when does my Haley girl not feel like steak?"

"I'm thinking about becoming a vegetarian." I don't know who's more shocked to hear that statement come out of my mouth, Mom, Lynn or me.

"A vegetarian?" Lynn and Mom say together, their eyebrows raised.

"Yep," I say nonchalantly. "I've been thinking about it for some time."

"What?" Lynn says, her voice a squeak. "You never mentioned it."

This is kind of fun in a perverse sort of way. I mean, I eat meat. Who am I kidding? I'm probably one of the biggest carnivores at our school. Refusing the steak was just another way to give Larry the finger. But now that I've announced it, seen the reactions, maybe I'll follow through with it. Buy myself some of those gross Birkenstocks and not wash my feet. Just joking. I won't go that far, but maybe I'll try to go vegetarian for a while.

"I've got secrets too," I say. Bad choice of words. I shouldn't have glanced up either. Would have missed Larry's wink.

Lynn's cell phone starts playing the ooh-ga-cha-cha song. "I'm sorry, Ms. Spence," Lynn says, smiling apologetically at my mom, scrabbling in her purse for her phone. "It could be my mom."

Bullshit. From the expression on her face, she's hoping it's Chad. Not to mention, she always checks call display, and when it's her mom on the phone, she lets voice mail answer. I wonder if that was what she was doing with me last night when I was trying to get a hold of her. I wonder if I'm now in the same don't-pick-up-the-phone category as her mom.

"Hello?" Lynn says breathlessly. She listens, a smile blossoming across her face. She covers the mouthpiece with her hand. "It's Chad," she whispers excitedly as she pushes away from the table and goes to stand over by the barbecue. I don't know why she bothers. It's only a few feet away. We can hear her clear as day. "Uh-huh. Uh-huh. Okay. That sounds good. Okay. Okay." Wow, they're having a real scintillating conversation. "Uh-huh. Okay. See you soon. Bye."

"See you soon?" I say the minute she hangs up. "What do you mean, see you soon? I thought you were sleeping over?"

"I am. I was," Lynn says, all flustered. "I mean, maybe I'm sleeping over. I'm not sure."

"You're not sure?" I don't know why I'm feeling so jealous. It's not like I like Lynn in that way or anything. Definitely not. So what's the big deal? Except it is. "I don't understand. Either you're sleeping over tonight or you're not!"

"I don't know yet. We're going to go over to Mike's place to hang out."

"Who's Mike?"

"One of his friends."

"So let me get this straight. Even though we're best friends, and we've made plans, you're going to blow me off —*again*—and go over to this Mike guy's house. Who you don't even know—"

"I met him last night—"

I railroad right over her. "—to hang out with Chad. A guy you've known for what? All of two weeks?"

"Well," Lynn says, like she's not sure what I'm getting so crazy about, "I was hoping you were going to come with me."

"What?" I'm stunned. She wants me to come. A smile starts spreading across my face.

"Yeah. Mike is a really nice guy. I think you would like him. Cute too. And Chad says he doesn't have a girlfriend, so I thought…"

"I don't know if it's such a good idea," Larry says, cutting her off. Like it's any of his business. "What do you know about these guys?" he asks my mom. His voice is sounding kind of belligerent. "Do you think it's safe?" Safe? Don't even get me started on safe! What a creep.

"Oh," Mom says, pushing back in her chair a little bit. "I'm sure they'll be fine."

"Are they going to be chaperoned?"

I can't believe he's acting so pushy. It's not like he's my dad or anything.

Chaperoned? Lynn mouths at me, rolling her eyes like, Is this guy cuckoo or what?

Mom looks at him for a moment. I'm not sure what she's thinking. I see a flash of something. I don't know what. It's gone a second later. Mom turns to me. "Are there going to be chaperones, honey?"

"I don't know. Are there?" I ask Lynn.

"Maybe," Lynn says, but I can tell she's lying. I think Mom can tell too.

Mom looks at me a long time, like she's adding up numbers in her head. "You'll be careful, Haley? Use good judgment?"

"Of course, Mom."

"No smoking marijuana."

"Mom, I told you before, I'm not…"

Lynn starts laughing because she thinks my mom's making a joke. "Yeah. Good one, Ms. Spence. Haley, smoking marijuana! That would be the day."

The frown wrinkles erase from Mom's forehead. She smiles, like she's relieved. "And bring your cell phone so you can call me if things get out of hand or you need a ride home." I nod.

"I'll give her a ride home, Ms. Spence," Lynn says.

"I really don't think Haley hanging out with these boys, without a chaperone, is a wise idea," Larry interjects.

Mom ignores him. "Okay," she says to me, her voice firm, like it's the end of the conversation. "You can go."

Chapter Sixteen

I'm sitting on the sofa with Mike. Apparently this is his apartment. He shares it with Ben. We're the only ones left in the living room. Sadie and Ben disappeared into Ben's bedroom, and Lynn and Chad are borrowing Mike's. Lynn almost forgot to take her purse in, but I scooped it up and handed it to her. "Don't you want your gum?" I said. So even though Mike's a very boring guy, it's a good thing I came along. Because what good are condoms if you leave them on the coffee table in your purse?

This sofa is quite old, a faded gray plaid with thin, rust-colored stripes. It's a sort of scratchy material, with about a million knobby fabric pills on it. When I first got here I was nervous. I wasn't paying attention to what my hands were doing, and I pulled off a couple of the pills by accident. Luckily, I caught myself and stuffed the evidence in the front pocket of my jeans before anybody noticed.

"Yes!" Mike yells, pumping his fist in the air. He turns to high-five me. I high-five him back. I guess the Canucks scored again. The announcer's saying something about Henrik Sedin, whoever that is. Must be one of the players.

"Is this a great game or what?" Mike says happily.

Now if it was Lynn and me sitting here, I'd say, "or what," but I don't think Mike would get my humor. Personally, I don't get the attraction of hockey. It's hard to see where the puck is on the TV, and all these little figures are racing around the ice, beating each other up. It seems like a lot of energy just to try to get the little black puck past the guy in the net. Big deal. And another thing that I find hard to watch is all the spitting. Like really, is that necessary? You're on national TV. Do we really need to see snotty mucus streaming from your mouth? No matter. I'm a guest in this guy's apartment.

"Yeah," I say, "it's great."

The TV goes to commercial. Mike leans forward to get himself a handful of chips that are lying on the coffee table. It's a good thing I brought them, because it's the only snack out. This guy doesn't eat them one by one like I do. He rolls them around in his hand for a second and then tips his head back and pours the whole handful in. I wonder if he practiced that. Maybe he thinks it looks manly or something. Like, hey baby, look how many chips I can fit into my mouth in one fell swoop.

Once the handful of chips has been dealt with, he stretches, and next thing I know his arm lands around my shoulders. I'm not sure what to do. So I just sit there, looking at the TV like this beer commercial is the funniest thing I've ever seen.

"I could use a beer," Mike says.

"Yeah, me too," I say.

I'm just making conversation, but I guess Mike doesn't know that, because he gets up, disappears around the kitchen divider and comes back looking pleased, two cans of beer in his hand. He pops one open, hands it to me and then sits down even closer, so our thighs are touching. He opens his beer, replaces his other arm around my shoulders and takes a long slurp. I take a sip, but I hold the beer tipped up to my mouth for a little bit longer so it looks like I'm drinking it properly. I don't really like the taste of beer.

I hear a moan come from Mike's bedroom. I hope it's a good kind of moan and not a *that-is-really-hurting* one. I've heard it sometimes hurts the first time you do it. I wonder if they're doing it or if they're just fooling around. That would be weird. Me sitting here on the sofa, watching the Canucks, while Lynn loses her virginity.

The commercial is over and the hockey players are whizzing around the rink. I guess this must be some pretty exciting game because Mike's hands are a little bit sweaty. My shoulder, where his hand is resting, is sort of moist and warm.

"Aw…Damn," he says. Somebody on the ice has done something wrong.

"What?" I say.

"Penalty," he says. His eyes are fixed on the TV. But I feel his hand start to move on a downward trajectory toward my breast, and my heart starts pounding.

I don't know what to do. His hand's almost touching my breast, but it's really confusing because it's his hand, some friend of Chad's, but it gets all mixed up with Larry, what happened with him. And I can't breathe. It's like Larry's got his hands wrapped around my throat again.

"Don't…" I say, my voice coming out barely a whisper. "Don't…please don't…"

Mike's hand stops. Everything stops.

"Are you crying?" he says.

I'm still watching the TV, but I can feel his eyes on me.

"Haley." He turns my chin toward him, gently. Looks into my face. "Are you okay? I'm sorry. Was I moving too fast?" And his kindness makes me cry even more.

"No, I'm sorry," I say. "I don't know why I'm crying." He goes to the bathroom and comes back with a roll of toilet paper.

"Here," he says. I blow my nose. It's funny, I never thought I'd ever blow my nose in front of a guy. But he doesn't reel back in horror and disgust. "Give it to me," he says, holding out his hand. "I'll put it in the garbage."

"Ew…no," I say, really embarrassed. "I don't want you to have to touch it." There's cheering on the TV. A big horn's blowing, so someone's scored, but he doesn't even glance at the television.

He's too busy taking care of me. He unrolls a few loops of toilet paper, lays them on his palm, holds it back out.

"There," he says, like the problem's solved. "Now I won't touch it."

I feel self-conscious, but I put my used toilet paper in his hand and he goes back into the kitchen to dump it. I can't believe he's so sweet. I can't believe I thought he was a big snore-fest.

He comes back into the living area and sits down. "Are you okay now?" he says, giving my hand a gentle pat. I never noticed that he had such nice brown eyes. His eyelashes are thick and long. There is something about the way he's looking at me that reminds me of a puppy.

"Yeah, I'm fine," I say.

"You sure?"

"I'm sure." We smile. We both turn back to the TV, but I keep my hand under his. And then, after a few minutes, I turn it over so we're holding hands. My hand in his. His hand in mine. We watch the rest of the game like that.

Once, in a commercial break, he brings our hands up, fingers still entwined, and brushes his knuckles softly against my cheek. It's really special. I don't want the night to ever end. But eventually the hockey game's over. The Canucks win in a shootout, four to three. Chad and Lynn emerge from the bedroom. I can't tell if Lynn's done it or not, but she looks quite tousled and her cheeks are flushed.

Mike and Chad walk us out to Lynn's car. Mike and I are still holding hands. It's a really nice feeling. Lynn and Chad start indulging in a major, full-body lip lock, up against the driver's door.

"Good night," Mike says.

"Night," I say, suddenly shy.

"Can I see you again?" he asks.

"I'd like that," I say.

Mike hesitates, then he leans in and gives me a hug. I hug him back. It feels good. I'd kiss him right now if he tried. But he doesn't. Just opens my door and I get inside. Lynn gets inside, starts up her car, slips in a CD and rolls her window down so they can hear the music too.

"See you tomorrow," Lynn calls out the window to Chad. We wave, they wave, as Lynn pulls away from the curb. I want to turn around and watch them walk back into the building, but I don't.

Chapter Seventeen

When we pull up to my house, all the lights are blazing. Which is odd. It's after eleven. Mom's usually in bed by now. The good news is I won't have to deal with Larry. His car's not in the drive, so he must have gone home.

"Wonder what's going on," Lynn says as she puts the car in park and sets the emergency brake.

"I don't know," I say, but my stomach's not feeling particularly settled. "Maybe you better not come in."

"But I was going to sleep over."

"I know," I say. "But maybe you better not."

Mom steps out onto the porch, her terrycloth robe tight around her to keep the late-night chill away. Her arms are crossed in front of her chest. This is not a good stance for her to be in. This is her you're-in-big-trouble-young-lady stance.

"Yeah," I say, my nerves rising to my throat. "I definitely think you should go home. She's pissed." I can't see her foot, because it's outside the pool of light she's standing in, but I'd bet good money that it's tapping.

"Okay," Lynn says. "I wonder what she's mad about."

"I don't know," I say, but I do. That asshole, Larry, must have filled her ear with a bunch of lies. I can only hope that she'll believe me when I tell her the truth.

I get out of the car. It's like I'm watching someone else move my body.

I hear Lynn say, "Call me when it's over. I'll put my cell on vibrate so it won't wake my mom." I feel my head nod. I start walking toward the porch. I can see my mom's eyes flashing fire from here. I keep walking. I hear Lynn's car reverse, back up and then head down the drive. I reach the porch. I climb the stairs.

"You have a lot of explaining to do, young woman," my mom says, her voice terse. "Inside. Right now." She holds open the door and I walk inside. The door slams shut behind me. The sudden adjustment, from darkness to the glaring brightness of the kitchen lights hurts my eyes.

Mom stalks past me to the living room. I follow. This is the room she always has the serious family meetings in. It is where she told me my grandfather had died. The one in which Mom and Dad informed me they had decided to get a divorce.

"Sit down," she says. I sit on the sofa. She doesn't sit. She paces in front of the night-filled picture window. She stops suddenly and turns to face me.

"I trusted you," she says, and I can hear the anguish in her voice.

"I know, Mom," I say. "I didn't mean to. Honest!"

"Didn't mean to? Ha!" She laughs, derisively. "What do you take me for? A fool?"

"Mom, *listen*. He came into my room. *Yes*, I invited him, but I thought it was you! I swear to God, Mom. I wasn't coming on to him. I don't even like him, for God's sake! You have to believe me."

And for the second time tonight, I find myself crying. Only this time, I'm crying hard. Choking on words and spit. "I never would want to hurt you, Mom. *Ever*. I don't know how it happened…"

"Wait. What are you talking about?" Mom's voice is sharp.

"Larry. That's why I locked my room. Not 'cause I was smoking p—"

"Back up! Back up!" My mom's on the sofa now. I feel her hands on my shoulders, shaking me slightly. "What are you talking about? Haley, honey, it's okay. Whatever it is, you can tell me." Her voice is softer now. I can see the edge of her chin as she bends a little, trying to look into my face.

"What…what were *you* talking about?" I'm suddenly so confused.

"I was talking about the condoms."

"The what?"

"The condoms, honey. The ones Sondra saw you buying at Shoppers Drug Mart this afternoon. Now, don't get me wrong. If you are having sex, I'm grateful that you are using condoms. It's just that…"

She breaks off. I glance up at her face, and it's like someone slugged me in the stomach. All of the sunshine from this afternoon has drained out and there is nothing left but this deep weary sadness.

"Now," she says, taking my hands in her soft, cool ones, "it's okay to tell me. It's important, baby. I need to know." Her gray-blue eyes catching and holding mine. "What happened with Larry?"